A Note to Parents

Reading books aloud and playing word games are two valuable ways parents can help their children learn to read. The easy-to-read stories in the **My First Hello Reader! With Flash Cards** series are designed to be enjoyed together. Six activity pages and 16 flash cards in each book help reinforce phonics, sight vocabulary, reading comprehension, and facility with language. Here are some ideas to develop your youngster's reading skills:

Reading with Your Child
- Read the story aloud to your child and look at the colorful illustrations together. Talk about the characters, setting, action, and descriptions. Help your child link the story to events in his or her own life.
- Read parts of the story and invite your child to fill in the missing parts. At first, pause to let your child "read" important last words in a line. Gradually, let your child supply more and more words or phrases. Then take turns reading every other line until your child can read the book independently.

Enjoying the Activity Pages
- Treat each activity as a game to be played for fun. Allow plenty of time to play.
- Read the introductory information aloud and make sure your child understands the directions.

Using the Flash Cards
- Read the words aloud with your child. Talk about the letters and sounds and meanings.
- Match the words on the flash cards with the words in the story.
- Help your child find words that begin with the same letter and sound, words that rhyme, and words with the same ending sound.
- Challenge your child to put flash cards together to make sentences from the story and create new sentences.

Above all else, make reading time together a fun time. Show your child that reading is a pleasant and meaningful activity. Be generous with your praise and know that, as your child's first and most important teacher, you are contributing immensely to his or her command of the printed word.

—Tina Thoburn, Ed.D.
Educational Consultant

For Jonathan—the Brat

No part of this publication may be reproduced in whole or in part, or stored in a retrieval system, or transmitted in any form or by any means, electronic, mechanical, photocopying, recording, or otherwise, without written permission of the publisher. For information regarding permission, write to Scholastic Inc., 555 Broadway, New York, NY 10012.

Library of Congress Cataloging-in-Publication Data

Hall, Kirsten.
  My brother, the brat / by Kirsten Hall ; illustrated by Joan Holub.
      p.   cm. — (My first hello reader!)
  "With flash cards."
  Summary: Two brothers discover that it can be fun to share their toys with each other.
  ISBN 0-590-48504-0
  [1. Brothers—Fiction.   2. Sharing—Fiction.   3. Stories in Rhyme.]
  I. Holub, Joan, ill.   II. Title.   III. Series.
  PZ8.3.H146My   1995
  [E]—dc20   94-32420
                                                                            CIP
                                                                             AC

12 11 10 9 8 7 6 5 4 3 2 1   5 6 7 8 9/9 0/0
                                                              24

Printed in the U.S.A.
First Scholastic printing, February 1995

MY BROTHER, THE BRAT

by Kirsten Hall
Illustrated by Joan Holub

My First Hello Reader!
With Flash Cards

SCHOLASTIC INC.

New York   Toronto   London   Auckland   Sydney

See my brother.

What a brat.

See him take my baseball bat!

See him take my choo-choo train.

See my brother.
What a pain!

I will take his
teddy bear.

I can take it?
You don't care?

see	take
my	baseball
brother	bat
him	train

we	your
choo-choo	it
I	truck
don't	pain

will	rubber
you	duck
what	can
a	care

fire	then
brat	share
his	teddy
little	bear

I can take your fire truck?

Then you can take my
rubber duck.

You can take it! I don't care!

Little brother, we can share.

Your Favorite Toy

What is your favorite toy?
Why is it your favorite toy?
How did you get this toy?
Did you pick it out?
Was it a present?

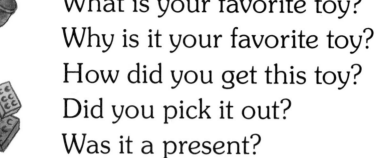

Rhyme Time

Rhyming words sound alike. For each word on the left, point to the word on the right that rhymes with it.

pain	my
duck	bat
I	truck
brat	train

Sports Fun

Point to the things that you would use for playing sports.

Now, point to the things that you would not use for playing sports.

Many Ways to Say It

Sometimes, a sentence has more than one meaning depending on how you say it. By changing your tone of voice or the look on your face, you can make a sentence mean different things.

Use your flash cards to spell out the sentence:

Little brother, we can share.

Say it out loud in a way that sounds friendly.

Say it out loud in a way that sounds like a question.

Now say the sentence another way.

Where's the B?

Some of these words start with the letter **b**. Some start with another letter. Point to the words that start with **b**.

baseball	brat
brother	pain
duck	bear
bat	truck

Clowning Around

Find the clown:

He is not wearing stripes.

He has purple shoes.

He is not wearing a hat.

He is not smiling.

Which one is he?

Answers

(*Your Favorite Toy*)

Answers will vary.

(*Rhyme Time*)

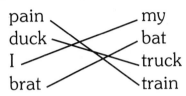

(*Sports Fun*)

You would use:

You would not use:

(*Many Ways to Say It*)

Answers will vary.

(*Where's the B?*)

baseball　　**brat**
brother　　**bear**
bat

(*Clowning Around*)

This is the clown: